KITSCH

The Little Things.

The Filthy,
Grotesque,
Inconsequential Little Things
That Make Life Interesting.

I Like To Collect Them,

Keep Them In A Jar By My Bed.

CHERYL ANNE GARDNER

KITSCH

A
Twisted Knickers
Publication

Kitsch

I like to go sit on the broken toilets near the drainage ditch and play the bongos — for the rats — in my underpants, while tapeworms turn filigree twists against the lining of my esophagus. I'd run out of toothpaste and soap ages ago, and once, I thought I saw Jesus in an old discarded power meter.

People like to throw things away: coffee pots, tomato soup cans, porno mags, and used asphalt stuck together with blonde hair, concrete, and ash. The blonde hair was attached to a gold pendant. It shimmered in the winter sunshine and caught my eye. It polished up real nice. Said *Faith* in thick fancy letters. I never wondered what it meant cuz people do that: they lose things, they find things, and they throw things away. The skulls get bleached out in the sun, and flies swarm out of the eye sockets, but after you boil them down a bit, clean them up a bit, they look kinda jazzy with some Christmas lights stuffed inside. I do that every once and a while, when I have gas for the generator.

The men who push the pipeline often ask me, why? Like there's some other place I should be. Maybe they were talking about the Christmas lights, I don't know. They come visit me, bring me beers sometimes. We sit around my little campfire until the vultures stop circling, and they tell me stories about gridlock and free upgrades and women with fake titties. They all worry about the cancer, and I look around me. In this place, the cancer eats through metal.

They call this place a dump. A place where the discarded come to die. I don't get insulted; last I checked, I was still breathing and taking pretty regular shits. "A man ain't a man without a good morning shit," I say, and they laugh and hand me another beer. Ask me if I'm afraid, their eyes rolling back over their shoulders as the darkness sets in.

Afraid of what? I always think. The rats? The mangy cats? Maybe it's the silence, but I don't remember ever being afraid of that. "It's just junk," I tell them, "and junk don't speak," then I smile at them, suck the air through the holes in my teeth, and hit on my bongos with a couple of shiny shinbones I found last week.

Broken

The way the moonlight struck her shoulder blades as she sat slumped over the table — face in a pile of blood and vomit — haunts me to this day. Maybe it was because I never trusted her, which was my only defense against the constant betrayals that she inflicted upon me. This was the worst by far. She'd said in her message that this night, the night I found her, would be something special. Something liberating, for the both of us. I was careful not to make any assumptions. She'd always said I assumed too much, expected too much. I think I understand what she meant now. Savage are those unsettling revelations that beg your attention at two A.M.

By the time I got there, it was hot in her apartment, stuffy, like the windows hadn't been opened in months. No air. No power. The refrigerator stank so bad from the outside, I didn't want to open it. The roaches swarming the pizza box on the counter were bad enough. Something smelled like eggrolls. Greasy dumpster cabbage. It's all borrowed time, I kept thinking, like yesterday when I pulled her pigtails at recess. We hadn't evolved much from that prepubescent tension. Not even after twenty years. A foggy twenty years of keyholes and sprockets and noisy snare drums. I leaned over and twisted the ribbon in her hair through my fingers. Even the watchers need to be watched, I thought. She'd always watched me, but I guess my eyes had wandered. I poured myself a glass of wine. The bottle was old, warm, and the liquid tasted of lint. I guzzled it down, then sat down, and told her she'd looked better. She always did, by candlelight. I lit a book of matches and tossed the flaming pile of sulfur and cardboard into the ashtray by her left arm, which was blackish blue in the dim light and covered in belt marks.

She'd ordered Chinese takeout. We'd do that sometimes — last night, last week … or maybe it was last year? We'd sit in the candlelight and sip wine. "What kind of life should we have?" she'd always ask with greasy *Kung Pao* chicken juice on her lips, and I'd sniff the spicy helplessness on her flesh before resuming the innocent caresses I used to placate her so often with. I never answered her. She had a haunting in her eyes that reflected back into you so deeply it was frightening, so my silence was never spiteful. She'd say, "There's no right or wrong way to feel about it," but the truth of the matter was, I just didn't know if there was any kind of life we could have.

Blowout

I was in way over my head. That's what I was thinking in the tense whiskey-fueled moments before I bled out and died. I wasn't thinking "Don't pull over," and I wasn't thinking about fine particulates or my asthma inhaler or the mummified remains of my boyfriend, which I had only just dug up from my backyard and placed in the trunk of my car. Probably a bad decision, since it's been so scorching hell-fire hot the past couple of days, but that's the thing, I hadn't thought about anything in weeks — years really — except that jughead in the trunk. I'd lost track of the time somewhere around Albuquerque in the 80s. I should have eased off the accelerator, should have known that the heat from the asphalt and the hail of rifle fire would blow out the tires. You'd be surprised how fast the details of your predicament emerge at one-hundred-sixty miles per hour in a shower of shattered glass. I WAS IN OVER MY HEAD. I knew this as I jerked the wheel and watched plastic Jesus fly off the dashboard with the wind in his hair and the stench of dry earth in my teeth.

Hula-hoops, Boys, and Bottle Rockets

S he didn't write about what I had said to her, or what I had done to her. She only wrote about who I would never be.

It was a summer day. "Hotter than hell-fire," mom said before she sent me into town on my bicycle. That's when I first seen her: the new girl. She was swinging her hips around the inside of a hula-hoop on the sidewalk in front of the local five and dime when I spotted her that first time. I thought she was a little flaky just standing there all alone swizzling that pink plastic around her tiny waste while the summer bees swarmed the bottle of soda she had left in the sun to get warm. I said "Hi," and she said "Hi" back, cracked her gum, and kept on swizzling. I was with the brass band at a school practice earlier. Was still in my uniform. It was itchy and tight, and I remember how small her toes looked in the little plastic grocery store flip-flops she was wearing. I remember thinking that bare feet were romantic. My mom had got me new shoes for practice. They were shiny, but they were tight and made my feet feel hot and cramped. I had to get the laundry at the *fluff and fold*. Mom would be angry if I came back late, wasted her time and her money if the clothes were crinkled up, but I couldn't stop staring at this girl. The hula-hoop had ball bearings or something inside of it, and it made this shucking sound as it swung in circles around her. With the laundry money, I thought, I could get us both some ice cream.

"Would you like some ice cream," I asked her. She didn't even look at me, just replied, "What kind?" and went on swinging, her tan summer toes gripping the concrete beneath her feet as if the hoop might spin her out into orbit.

"I don't know," I said. "Whatever kind you want, I suppose. We could go down to the marsh, sit in the shade for a bit."

"I don't go with boys," she said all matter of fact like, scrunching up her nose at my boy stink. But I wasn't a boy. Not in my uniform. Mom said I looked like a man in my uniform, so I told her that, pointed to all my shiny buttons and stuff. She smiled at me and said, "Ok." The marsh was warm, quiet, still, and she didn't scream that much when I hit her. It was really hot that day. I felt feverish. I don't remember what she'd said to me, or much after she said it, except her ice cream, melting clotted milk into the mud.

That girl doesn't hula-hoop outside of the five and dime anymore. I go there every day, and I wait, change for ice cream jingling in my pocket. I wait there alone; sometimes so long I forget what she looks like. I still see her most days though, at the back of the schoolyard, in the shadows, writing in her little book. She has this look in her eyes as she scratches and tears at the pages, and I just know she isn't writing about me.

Debt Collectors

'd taken about a hundred hits before my center gave way like blubber piled on a shit-stained mattress. I'd done the couch surfing dream sex thing to my father's porno mags; the bed-wetting thing, hunkered down against my mother's incessant prayers, which she thought would save my soul; hell, I even dragged in a few shaved cats when I was in college. Ma said I was blessed by the Devil, so blessed, I've had all the cancer therapy a person can stand before they start to feel suicidal. So here I sit, toking it up until I can hear my own voice echoing off the back of my head. A baseball game is being called out in earnest on the radio when the streetlights start to flicker. I don't notice right away because I'm sat here thinking about whether or not I had already put fresh brick dust across all the open doorways. "Dusk to dawn, dust them gone." Ma said that. Said the shadows were on the move. I can remember running down this very street as a kid, trying to hit the porch step before my pop came out and grounded me for being out after dark. "It's a simple thing," he used to say while running his fingers over his belt buckle. He'd had a metal plate in his head for a while, but the government replaced it with plastic. That's why I had to be inside before the streetlights came on. Before the shadows. Those lights were the only warning, Pop said, because he'd lost radio reception on account of the plastic, you see. He'd fought in THE WAR. Never said which one, never said he was afraid. Sometimes I thought he was still fighting it. He'd wring his hands a lot, and I heard him tell Ma once that he felt unclean. When he wasn't in the basement, he was on the porch. He'd sit and listen to the static on the radio for hours, his eyes focused hard on the dark just beyond the porch rail. He'd point every once and a while and say, "Look there boy!" and I would look, squint my eyes, but I wouldn't see anything even though I said that I had. "BASTARDS!" he called them. "Fascist F.A.G. f*!*ing ni**!rs," he'd say while chucking rocks into the darkness, and I thought his anger seemed kind of personal even though I didn't know what any of those words meant at the time. Now that I think about it, between the layers of smoke and the equally vague layers of pain, maybe it was personal — for him. Maybe those shadows weren't for me to see.

Pop didn't make it home one night before dark. He never came home. Ma blamed the shadows, and I didn't see them when they came for her either.

So now I sit here on this miserable-excuse-shanty-shack hunk of termite shit porch, nothing left of me but blanched skin. Ma's gone. Pop's gone. All I've got left is this dilapi-shack, Pop's hate, and that damn dirty basement. I take another toke on my cigarette and exhale just as the streetlights snap on. I know they're coming, can feel a tightening in my chest, so I reach down and turn the knob on the radio until I'm tuned into the static. Then I stare into the dark just beyond the porch rail …

I stare, and I stare, and I stare until I scream.

Long Island Iced Tea

The argyle socks intimidated me, the way they dimpled just below his big fat ankles. He wanted to swim with them on: *Aquaman* in bad leisurewear. There were some bricks lying around the pool, and I wanted to pick one up and heave it at his head. His father and his father before him were starting to show more and more on his face. Men that would never admit that they looked a fool in speedos and socks and sandals. I watched him walk over to the poolside, kneel down, and attempt to retrieve one of his sandals that had fallen into the water. He looked like a turnip with socks. Except that turnips don't have hairy butt cracks. I wanted to look away, but when I tried, I got a cocktail umbrella in my eye. I was feeling very slippery from the suntan lotion, so I didn't want to move my seat for the sake of changing the view. It didn't take more than fifteen minutes or so before he noticed me staring at him and decided he might take a shot. I couldn't really see his face all that well. He had a lot of gold chains snarled in the gray hair that was matted down with cocoa butter all over his flabby man-tits, and the reflection from the sun off the gold and greased blubber was blinding.

It was a weekend retreat: no deadlines, no budgets, no authority figures, and my horoscope said to accept any and all invitations offered, so when he said, "Would you like to accompany me to the buffet?" I thought shit, you are the buffet, honey, and then I wondered if his kidneys might taste good boiled or fried with or without onions and a little butter. Should I pickle his eyes, his ears, his nose, and his toes? We could decide all that later, after the salad I'd ordered, after a few generous glasses of strychnine-laced iced tea, and after the thin mint I'd have for dessert while chuckling silently at his red jiggling face, chewing and chewing and chewing, grease from the supersized burger he was eating dripping down his six chins. Through the partially digested cud in his mouth, he asked why women like me — you know, skinny — always ate rabbit food. I felt a gob of sinew hit my cheek as he laughed after he said he liked rabbit burgers. I told him, "Meat never sticks to me," but that he seemed like he had no trouble. He said dieting was the only thing he never had trouble with. I believed him. His neck was so thick. His muscles, I imagined, were marbled with nice creamy fat. He was huge, and it was then that I realized I might actually have trouble choking this one out.

Making Dinner on Mars

Have you ever smelled a burning body? After it'd gone black and cracklin' crispy, all hollow eye sockets and yellow teeth. I hadn't before that night, but Jerry felt he'd been undervalued as the local convict for far too long.

"Bunch a wing-backed crackers," he often called them. He'd warned them, all twenty-seven of them found stabbed, chunked, skewered, and BBQ grilled at the farm off Rural Route 2. They hadn't identified the beheaded woman yet, but one less obituary than he had wanted seemed like a fair deal. At that point, he'd have taken any deal at all. He swore up and down that he'd done the right thing. Done stopped a plague worse than the locusts we'd had the prior year. His hatred stank of porno and sweat, and the assault charges wouldn't have stuck if he hadn't decided, just that day, to snort a little graveyard dust before doing some recon inside that busted up mausoleum on the outskirts of town. He said it was where the monsters lived like in that damned stupid horror movie.

"Monsters," he'd said again with a drizzle of chaw spittle runnin' down his chin. "The ones that brought the rats in the corn."

We'd heard the rumors about the rats since we were kids, but that day, we were scared. Jerry was like a demented sleeper cell with smallpox. He carried an axe handle, sharpened to a point "Just in case" he had to stake one of them damned dirty nightwalkers before they got a chance to cross the border. He knew no one would ever call him a hero on account of his record and all, but he was brave that warm, still, moonless night, screaming like a banshee as he doused the dried out bodies with gasoline and watermelon flavored liqueur.

A Lukewarm Glass of Milk

She liked eating the lint she found under the furniture cushions. Liked chewing the paint off the bedpost when we made love. Everything was always beginning with her. Predawn. Fresh cut flowers sans the morning dew. She was double-jointed, and when she hit me, she said it was just a reflex.

"I can't find my jacket. You know, the brown one with the fancy leather flowers on the lapels," she said, then she gave me the stink eye as she cut a banana into her morning cereal.

The sun was just coming in through the kitchen window, and when it lit on her, her whole face sparkled from the pancake makeup she always applied too thickly. She said her life was in miniature, carved of Chinese jade then photographed in black and white and tacked to a light post in a parking lot. Everything was brilliant to her, always in the fake British accent she'd learned from watching too many foreign films. She sipped her coffee, said I wasn't flexible anymore. I told her, "The jacket is in the basement closet." I'd put it there because it stunk of cigarette smoke, even though she'd said she quit. The newspaper says the forecast for today will be hazy with a heat index of 101 degrees. I don't understand the heat index. How do they know how hot it feels to me?

Unexpected Guests

I can't get it to stop," my girl said softly, her hands clenching flesh, cartilage, and bone, and I just looked away, said nothing as the night silently slipped through her fingers. I wanted to say something, but this time, the disappointment kept me silent. This time, I'd lost my nerve to finish it. I don't know why. We'd danced this dance before, me and my girl. This time was no different. We saw the doorknob turn, heard the keys drop, saw the shuffling struggle to find them in the meager light streaming in under the door. They were drunk — Debbie and Dallas — pumped up on ecstasy, strobe lights, and a back alley blowjob. No, this time wasn't a rare occasion. We'd watched them from a virtual distance for some time. We'd lived vicariously through their tales of torture and slavery. We hated them their listlessness and pitied them their bedroom boredom. We'd watched them slide into dreams and the rotted sewer that is middleclass dementia. We'd even cheered for their hokey homemade porn: the way he knocked her senseless and the way she didn't care as long as her prescriptions got filled. Yes, we'd targeted them. They were careless.

But this night wasn't like all the others.

I remember my knees aching. No padding. Cheap carpet. It was a setup: bingo, AM radio, coconut daiquiris, and their even cheaper looking implants and painted on smiles. Though Debbie's melted right off her pasty face as soon as she saw us. As soon as she knew why we were really there.

"We've never done anything like this before," said the husband when he'd answered our personal ad: DEB-BIE AND DALLAS SEEKING A THRILL. Ha! They all say that ... and they all regret it after we've finished with them. This time the husband went too far. Poor Dallas. He'd lied a little. Liked it a little more than we had anticipated. He screamed. He pled for mercy. Eventually, he wept. That just turned my girl on more. The love of my life. She couldn't help herself. The smell of sweat and old leather mixed with hatred and fear. "Just a little nick," she'd said, so she could see what he was made of, and then poor Dallas stopped breathing.

"I can't get it to stop," my girl said again, more de-manding. We hadn't even done Debbie yet. I wanted to, but she was getting cold, and now we had to clean blood out of the carpet.

Espresso / Are These Beans Burnt? They Taste Burnt to Me.

They went to the same cafe every day. Sat there sipping the same lattes and reading the same books they had brought with them each and every time before. He always sat in the back of the room. She liked the window. Most afternoons, he wrote. She liked the way he held his pen. The way his writing looked effortless when she only ever struggled. She thought one day that he might look up at her in passing. She tried to order loud enough so that he could hear. She wanted it "Rich, and Thick, with lots of Sweet ... Buttery ... Foam." She licked her lips, thought of licking him. He looked over at her. That was the second time in a month. Did he know what she was thinking? Did he want to suck that latte foam off her mouth? Did he want her, right there on the table with the barista watching?

Yes ... he did.

He'd always wanted her, wanted to dribble steaming hot milk on her stomach until it boiled her flesh inside out. He wanted to shove pastry up her ass with his leather-clad fist. He imagined her insides tasted gooey like sugary-cream-salted taffy left out in the sun. He smiled at her. Adjusted his pants. Went back to writing. He imagined her in just her lacey black panties. He had looked, once, and seen them when she crossed her legs.

She wore those stockings, the kind with garters. He wanted to cut them off slow with the straight razor he had in his pocket, wanted to wrap them around her throat while he kissed her gasping red mouth. She was so sexy. He imagined she'd scream, slap his face. He imagined she wanted him like that, her chest flushed and heaving, glass breaking all around them. He could feel the sweat against the hair on his legs.

"Sir."

He wanted her, all of her — her meat, her organs, and her pretty blue eyes — and he wanted her to want him. Wanted her to beg for it until she couldn't take it anymore.

"Sir."

He wanted those gorgeous latte covered lips, face down now, heels up later in the dumpster.

"Sir! ... Do you need anything else?"

He put his pen down, took his glasses off, and wiped the sweat from the lenses. He looked over at her. She was still smiling at him.

"Yes," he replied to the waiter. "Can I have some very hot milk? To go."

Glass Houses

Y ou gonna throw that?

Throw what?

Oh come on, that fucking rock right next to you.

Maybe.

You promised you wouldn't.

When the hell did I say that?

Yesterday. You remember our conversation from yesterday, right? You promised you would never do it again.

No I didn't. I never said any such thing.

I fucking heard you.

You don't listen to me. You never have. You just hear what you want to hear.

No I don't.

Yes you do.

No ... you say shit to shut me up.

No I don't. I don't say shit at all.

Yes you do. You make shit up and then you say it like you mean it, but you don't.

I don't say "shit." I say what I mean.

No, you say what you think it means.

Well I can't very well say something someone else

thinks it means, now can I? This is absolutely ridiculous. Why are we arguing about this stupid shit?

So I'm stupid then?

Oh, for fuck sake. I said "stupid shit" not "you're a stupid shit."

But you were thinking it.

I'm not talking about this anymore.

That's because you don't want to hear me.

I'm not talking ...

***

So, you gonna throw that too?

What?

That fucking stick.

No.

No what?

No ... I'm gonna poke you in the eye with it.

Ditch Diggers Tend Picket Fences

Silence spreads into space, upstream in nuclear steel and chrome comfort. There's a bottle of gin on the floor that should be empty but it's not, and an argument under the table that shouldn't be but is. He'd tried to escape but couldn't, and she asked for it — with question marks. Told him that his ellipses were obscene, and then she cried briefly to survive him. "So I'll stay," he said, again, and she told him to bury it out next to the shed. There's a maple tree there, listing against the wind, so he put on his gumboots and carried it out there alone with gin hands bare. Shaking. The shed door rots, protests, and the coal shovel's rusted out. A life lived in short seasons, he thinks as he stabs the earth with a clank only to realize that he couldn't break ground even if he tried, and he's tried so many times, but the soil is sour. She knows that. The daisies she plants die every year. She won't be perfect or right or wonderful, he will never not be ignorant, and the daisies will always fucking die. Without argument. Without question marks.

Once, he painted a green field, she standing in it, the wind in her hair and in the lace hems of her dress. She cut the skin from her breast and gave it to him. He set his hair on fire and gave her the ash. They made love in the moonlight, that field now gray, and as he pressed his thumbs into her throat, she asked him a question, but he can't remember what it was. Then she said she wished she had a glass eye, one that would never grow hazy when she looked at him, like the marbles they'd played with on the street when they were kids. He had one in his pocket just for such an occasion. She laughed and she laughed, and she laughed … until she didn't.

It used to be you and me.

We.

Us.

Now it's just he. She. Them. Always kneeling there, under that tree in the dead dirt, praying for something… anything at all. Hoping for an emptiness she can live with: a hole deep enough for all his regret.

Sometimes Things Just Are What They Are

The bowl on the rest stop sink was full of potpourri. I put my gun in my coat pocket. The potpourri smelled of cinnamon, my hands smelled of gunpowder, and as I looked in the mirror above the sink, I couldn't help thinking about Christmas.

Sam had got his wife a diamond bracelet. He got me a bag of coke. He'd said that she'd "never had rich stuff before." He smiled thoughtfully when he said it, sipped his coffee with a lit cigarette in a shaky left hand. When we left the diner, I thanked him for the coke, smiled at him, and then I put a bullet in his head. It was midnight, and the moon was out. As I walked over his body, I noticed tinsel on his lapel. It didn't concern me beyond the fact that I noticed it. What did concern me was the lipstick on his collar, which I knew wasn't his wife's. She doesn't wear lipstick, or perfume ... or panties for that matter.

Gourmet Meat Haters

B e yourself." That's what my girl always said to me just before I'd get my game on. Leather straps, chain mail, stainless steel studded gloves, it was the future of sport, and I was a gladiator in the making. We were waiting, parked on the side of the road. I'd just finished my beer and tossed the can out the window. My girl didn't want to hit it just yet. The *Bangles* were on the radio, and she hadn't quite finished butchering the lyrics. Her toenails were painted — deep blood red with a glittery candy swirl — and her legs were smooth in those ragged denim shorts. I could see her pubic hair busting out at the seams.

Her hands were dirty.

She was dirty.

She flicked a cigarette ash out the window, and the lit embers got caught in the breeze. It was one of those soft summer nights. Silent. Still. Just after a thunderstorm. Crickets chirping in the tall grass. I liked to watch her take a piss in the weeds on the side of the road after we'd finished digging the graves. Some say we got lost. Stopped dreaming. I didn't think so. The blood looked black on my hands. We'd crossed over somewhere in the last few months. Me and my girl. Exhumed each other's rotted corpses. If you'd asked me about it a month or so ago, I'd have said we weren't going to make it. "Scraped out," she'd said when I'd asked her about it, but somehow, I don't know, we got wise, I suppose. Stopped gnawing on the foil, waiting for a spark. "Pamplona," she'd said with a pouty smile that hid all the gaping holes from the teeth she'd had knocked out. It was only a suggestion, but I'm highly susceptible to suggestions, so we hauled ass. Ditched it. Swapped out the organic dogshit pate and health food stores for toxic porn and tent city freak shows. God damn! Her skin was so soft and pale in the moonlight, her eyes so dead.

"I love you," she'd said after the charges were dropped the first time.

It wasn't so much that she'd said it. It was the way she'd said it, like a vaccine tapped in a dry vein. She'd punish me for what I'd done.

Eventually.

What Do We Do With The Silence?

A light wind swept through the greasy strands of her hair, and the sunshine just laughed at her. She said she didn't remember me.

"But I loved you," I said, to which she replied that love was a terminal indignity; then she reached in through the open window and flicked her cigarette ash on the seat of my car as if she were lobbing a grenade. The burning ember scorched a hole in the leather, and she said she was cheaper than it would cost to fix the upholstery.

I didn't care what she cost. I thought she was brave, braver than I ever was — living amongst the corpses — the spring rains bringing only pain to the sisters swapping passports on the street corner. I don't know, it seemed like fair trade to me: a prayer for the weight of her worry, so I asked again, "What's your worry, girl?" but this time, she didn't answer. She must have remembered that I'd asked her that once before, in the dark of a confessional. Asked her if she watched the toaster-oven with ice crystals sculpting her hair? She'd said she had, that she liked to stick a fork in the red-hot coils. She called me her piano man then, and I'd wondered how many others she had.

I asked her, "Do you kiss the piano men ... on the mouth?"

And she said, yes.

"How does it make you feel ... sick?"

She said, no.

How then? I'd wondered.

They taste good, was her reply.

"So how does it make you feel ... when you taste them?" Only this time, she refused me, picked at her fingers, and I knew, then, that it made her feel warm and tingly and a little dizzy in the knees. Like God ... Like Love.

"Do you love them ... these piano men?" I'd thought she might, but she'd said, no. It was a No with a question mark, so I didn't believe her. It seemed so cold when she said it.

NO, she said again. *I love only you.*

I told her I played the clarinet not the piano, and she laughed at me. It was a laugh that had made me forget about the world outside. A laugh that had me pause before I asked if all the piano men came to her like this: like me. Of course, she'd said, yes, and I can remember wondering if they called her babe before they set the clock radio next to the bed in the burned out hotel room she called home. Again, she said, yes.

It's digital. They set it for their escape.

And I asked, "Theirs, not yours?" but she didn't answer. She just smiled, red chalky lipstick scraping against dry teeth.

She had that same lipstick on now, and it rippled like the heat off the pavement. I tugged at the white plastic pressing against my throat and asked her for a cigarette.

She said, no, that I was chronic, that I had no originality, so I told her I thought the sky was going to change. Not today, but maybe tomorrow: the rain would come. She just looked up into the sun, lit another cigarette, and blew the smoke directly into my face. She said she didn't mind the winter rains, said the sun was rough, sharp-toothed, and she was right. I could see the creases in her skin now, and how the solar flares off the hot tin roof behind her had satisfied themselves once, politely, in her bleached-out frizzy hair. I rolled up the window, pulled away from the curb. They didn't need her like I did. Didn't want her like I did. Didn't have to have her like I did, but I would try not to think about her, would go about my days, keeping her close in the silence ... until the cold came ... until I knew I could be her confessor again.

In the dark.

In the icy rain.

Parachuting in Stilettos

t had finally hit the triple digits, and the beach looked like a garlic pizza with roasted humans on top. While I was snoozing in the sun, I had this bizarre dream of a glass lemon hanging in the air above my head as a waiter dressed in black-tie towered over me reciting a menu in French. When I opened my eyes, an oily bohunk in a slinky banana-hammock was standing over me. He was so greasy, he could have slipped, nipples first, into another dimension. He had a fistful of sand, which he proceeded to fling into my face. I spit some exorcism in pig-Latin at him, and he smiled, then asked me if I wanted to go dancing. I told him to "fuck off," so he left only to return five minutes later with a *pina-colada* that had an umbrella in it so huge that it eclipsed the sun.

I really did want to go dancing, but my feet had always been too big for high heels. I can clunk, I can funk, I can jump strapless off the shoulders of a naked barista ... but I can't glide in them enough to dance.

Taking Lives

Mother always said, "Never take what isn't yours." She had a big mouth, so I took her tongue. She fought me something awful, kicking, biting, screaming shit at me. She damn near took my eye out with a ballpoint pen she always kept stashed in her bra. When she finally calmed down, I had to explain things to her. By that point, she couldn't really argue semantics with me anymore.

When I was a kid, I got caught stealing a lot. When I did, I'd sit in my room, in the corner, in the shadows ... waiting for her. I might sit there for hours, sometimes days, hoping I could make myself so small and insignificant that I would disappear into the wallpaper or the dust on the floor. When she came for me — and she would eventually come for me — I would hear her, switch in her hand, flick flick flicking against the wall ever so lightly, collecting cobwebs in its wake as she approached my bedroom door.

I'm not a kid anymore.

I like taking things. I like it a lot.

When I take your skin, I promise I'll only take a little at time ... just enough for you to feel it. I'll take it first from somewhere no one will notice. It'll be our secret — the hurt. Then we'll talk a bit. Converse. There's so many things: breast implants, mercury poisoning, and drug free meat. There's this tension between us. I like that. We agree to disagree. I want to savor this moment so that when I take the hurt, cut through the muscles and the sinew, you'll know it and accept it — the hate.

Eventually, I'll take that too. When I reach inside for its pulsating mass, you'll beg a little and say that you don't, but I know you do. I'll explain things to you, that you don't have to hate me, hate anything for that matter. You need to let it go. If you don't, I'll just take it anyway, and when I do, you'll admit you were wrong and that I was right all along.

I like taking things.

Especially when mother is watching.

Candlelight Vigils

H e crept down the clanking steel, whipping the bare skin of his calf with the leather belt on his trench coat each step he took. "Therapy," he kept telling himself as he counted the steps, and would, maybe later, the strike marks left upon his skin; though in the daylight, the red never looked red enough, never felt deep enough. His vision of life as he knew it had become a tatty film reel — black and white — silent and uncut – click, click, clicking off in the periphery like someone else's memories.

Or maybe they were his. He couldn't be sure. Not anymore.

He left work that day — alone — with an umbrella — open — his knuckles chalky-white as evidence of how hard the wind was blowing the rain into his face. Mascara running down his cheeks, pale skin blossoming in the florescent lights, he would escape the world of black and white, the world of men, of suits and ties and lies. He would escape underground where private conversations echoed back against damp tile walls, where bargain hunters in bare feet traded *Fritos* for anatomy lessons. "I love you," he said, quietly, just barely an audible whisper above the sounds of retching and grunting. A beggar tugged at his purse in the dark, and he remembered why he was there, why he had come here, and why he was waiting.

He'd said the "L" word once. Meant it once, when he'd said it to himself in the mirror — 6:00 a.m. — when the morning light through the bathroom window at his flat was too weak to reach into the corners, but that was long ago, before the moths got to the silk, before the hems tattered. His lover had given him a string of pearls then, back then when he could grab and touch the bashful passage that was the woman he knew as himself.

A train would eventually come. He knew it, so he waited, and when it did, he would slip ... out of his heels. When he could feel the ground rumbling. When he could smell his own perfume over the grease from the rails.

Skinned Rabbits

She was a social climber, glamorous — a feminist in her own mind — and she loved the hunts out at the lake. She loved the eerie glow of the moonlight, the way it broke apart and came back together in the ripples of black water, and she loved the way a shotgun shell felt when palmed in her hand. An opportunist, she smiled and said, "Yes" when I offered to buy her a drink. She was the only one sitting at the bar that night, and I fell in love with the way the cigarette smoke parted her lips when she drew out the *sssss* in yes. Her makeup was a little theatrical around the eyes, and she smelled a bit boozy and a little stale when she crossed her legs, but hanging around the likes of bars like these will do that to a person. Mattresses get stained. I should know. I had one in the back of my van, not for just such an occasion. I found myself homeless a lot. Not a crisis, and I never tried to hide behind anything or anybody. The blame fell square at my own two cowboy-cake coated feet. She'd have found me anyway. I had trouble centering myself in the world. Took liberties, that sort of thing. I didn't used to be, but now I am: a thief, a swindler, a panhandler planning to raid a dead woman's womb, a live grenade in one hand, a roasted squirrel on a stick in the other. She didn't know that though. She was too drunk, and I was wearing my good flannel.

"Whattcha got in the knapsack?" she asked, and I wasn't really sure what to tell her. There was some bathroom tile from a public restroom, a couple unused rail tickets, the *Shondells* on compact disc, and a gray crayon. "Memories," I suppose is what I thought I said loud enough to be heard over her curiosity and the jukebox.

"Shame," she replied, "I was looking for porcelain. You know: a white rabbit, maybe. Something small ... for my kid."

"You got a kid?"

"Yes ... Well, no. Sometimes. He likes rabbits."

Run Rabbit Run, was all I kept thinking as her voice droned on and on and on.

She said she lived where the rocks were sharp and coyotes howled in the night. There were no rabbits. She said she had tried to paint them, once, so her kid could believe in them.

She looked too old for a kid, too used. She smiled again, went to push her crispy hair back behind her ear. She didn't give it much thought when the strand she was playing with hit the tip of her cigarette and caught fire, curled up, and fell in small ashes on her collar, and I didn't give it much thought when I noticed the lampblack on her knees and the matchbox full of fingernails, which she had labeled "divine" in red polish and sparkling pink paint. *Run Rabbit Run,* was all I kept thinking ... until the thinking stopped. I don't remember much after the fifth shot of tequila, what happened to my clothes, or even if we'd ever made it back to my van. I taste iron in my mouth; spit dirt. It's so very, very, cold — dark — and more cold, and the sound of shotgun blasts echoing closer and closer in the distant darkness is worse than the howl of the coyotes and the ache of my bare and bloodied feet.

Run Rabbit Run, was all I kept thinking as my frozen balls crept up into my ass...

This is your last chance to — Run.

The Mission Box

D ark and damp and so very cold, the air sits still over, around, and through me. Smells like old and dirt and mold. Sometimes I scratch and scream. Sometimes I lay quiet; pick little flakes off charred sky with my fingernails; feel them hit my face and my hair. I know I must, and so I try to breathe shallow until morning, when I think it might be morning, when the rain comes soaking its way through and makes the air taste like sweat and rust, makes the hinges squeal in the lost dead hours I wish I'd forgotten.

He knows my name, but never says it.

Knows that my eyes ache from reaching into the shadows, but he doesn't care.

He'll never care.

He says he knows what misery looks like, and that I'm not quite there yet, haven't surrender to it yet, not fully, not the way he wants. He says that my sickness is genetic, not a cancer, so my treatment must be slow and meticulously thought out.

He thinks a lot.

Talks a lot.

Sometimes too much for me to bear.

I imagine he must have a deep crease in his brow and coal-black penetrating eyes. That his hands are thin, pale — slight — able to set things in motion. Able to put things right.

I never see him, even when the darkness abates and the light shines strong into my eyes.

I never feel him, even when he touches me in places he shouldn't dare.

I always hope for a spring breeze or a winter's frost but never smell anything beyond the bleach, the rubber, and the moist rot of old wood around me.

I hope for the stars; the moon; the dew-drenched chicory underfoot in an abandoned field, toasting in the midsummer sun. I hope for the smell of bacon and eggs on a Sunday morning; the way my dad sips his coffee, crinkles his newspaper; and the way mom smells of laundry soap when you press your face into her apron. The softness of her abdomen. The softness of her voice. Not like his.

He couldn't save the others, he said, and I knew he wasn't lying about that. I could hear the hammer strike iron. A thousand times I could hear it. Could hear the drag of emptiness against dirt. His feat shuffling against the weight. There'd be no more whispers now. No more tears but mine, and so I wait: days, months, years … seasons, sunsets, holidays … shouldn't talk to strangers … Blah, Blah, Blah. This is the minutia that is me, he says in our therapy sessions when he speaks to me through the darkness, through pinpricks, and curses, and infatuations … stupid stupid stupid … the sutures never hold. No. He couldn't save the others, but if he can isolate it — If he can, he says — he just might make it his mission to save me for someone.

Someone other than himself.

The LongPig

He wasn't trying to kill me. Didn't have a taste for me, he said, grease dripping through bloody gristle down his fat and scrumptiously bare tits.

I could never rely on anyone to look out for me. Not now. Not when I was a kid. Couldn't rely on anyone to stand up, to protect. It was a shame, really, just a damn shame: crying alone, feeling ugly, measured in slights and trifles, until I met him.

YOU MUST BE 18 OR OLDER TO JOIN.

So what! I contemplate. I Annex. Then I plunge. Head-first? Maybe. So what, so what, so what …

Hey there, Puppet!

Hey there to you too, not your real name either.

You're funny, kid. How old are you?

Old enough!

Old enough, huh? Wanna play a game then?

What kind of game? Subterfuge Twister? Where's Mr. Mephistopheles in gingham and rubber pants?

Yeah, whatever, kid. You bet.

I'm bored, obviously, so it had better be good.

You won't be bored, kid.

You sure?

Yes. I like you, kid, and nobody I know dies of boredom.

Sounds refreshing.

It is, kid. It is. Trust me.

Don't know you. Can't really trust you.

I know. Exciting, isn't it?

Yeah, kinda.

So what do you say, kid? Are you in?

Yes.

Yes, what?

Yes. I'm in.

He asked if I liked to eat, said he liked to cook for people who liked to eat. Liked to prepare things to be eaten. He sent me pictures: Lean cuts. Nicely marbled. Slabs pink, seasoned, and tenderized. Fresh. Fed on sunshine and green grass. He said he worked in an abattoir: Cages. Tables. Scalpels. Freezers. Steel on Steel on Steel. Didn't contaminate the meat, he said. I thought that was good — at first. At first is a funny thing. Never means what it is in the end. We ignore things at first.

We don't mind.
Want a friend.
Feel Desperate.
Feel Lonely.
STARVING.

No, we don't mind a lot — at first. Charity. Oversight. Whatever. Then we see things we don't want to see.

Things we can't unsee.

Then *at first* becomes something else. Something needful, dark, and horrible. Something so satisfying. So right.

He wasn't trying to kill me, at first, but when he wasn't, I was trying to kill him.

Gekkonidae

He liked to go places he wasn't allowed to go. Dark alleys. Unlocked stairwells. The backs of parking lots where they keep the dumpsters, and the basement. He liked to pretend he belonged to this or that other person, was the long lost son, found after years of searching, or was the beloved special child who won awards and trophies and would make them proud someday despite his handicap. He didn't like cream of wheat or wearing sandals on the beach because of broken glass or other stuff that could puncture his skin. He didn't really like the beach at all. He liked to pretend to make tea in his room for his sister's dolls. She liked it too; though he was convinced his sister wasn't really human and didn't belong in the family he didn't like very much anyway. His grandma's ashes were on the mantle in a terracotta vessel. His mom called it that, but it looked more like a plain ole jar to him. Someday he'd break that jar and grind the ashes into the carpet. He'd do that soon because any minute, he might change into a reptile with shiny skin and a grand smile and a long tail that had a kink in the tip. If he were a reptile, ladies at the grocery store would caress him and say, "I thought he would be slimy." Then on the way home from the store, he'd break all the eggs in the grocery bag when his mom was yelling and paying attention to the road. She was an executive something or another, took power naps when her eyes got weary from looking at him. She drank holy water with rocks in the bottom, and dad surfed the net, jumping up with a poodle-howl whenever someone said something he didn't agree with. Which was a lot. Moss is green. It grows on the back stoop where the spigot drips on the brick like a blessing. He thought he might become a saint someday maybe, eat caviar and bananas and wear a bejeweled hat on his head, and he'd live in a tree fort lost in the woods somewhere where there weren't any people to tell him what to do. Till then, he wanted chicken nuggets and soda and a dime he could stick in the electrical socket by the boy's bed that wasn't his bed.

Just to see what happens.

Under New Management

You always liked the color of your nose, raspberry red. It matched the glittery dazzle of your rainbow hair when the neon lights hit it just right, and man did they always hit it just right, the vibrant honey-yellow big-bird frizz and feathers, swaying to and fro as you tripped and stumbled in your oversize shoes. Those were the days, all sungold and velvet stardust. That was until the thugs came, with their gold teeth and their tainted food, all "step right up" like cherry liqueur and melted sugar. Somehow, somewhere, you'd dropped your compass. It was eight below that night, the last night you would ride your tricycle under the spotlight in the rain.

Communion

I dream empty, the wind blowing benzene blue.
Shards of glass.
Barbed wire.
Bricks crushing flame into notions gone quick,
Never painless.
Is it my blood?
In my eyes.
On my hands.
Is it for you?

       I'm not sure where I'm walking here.
          Walking towards what from.

Is it supposed to be like this?
I don't think so,
Don't imagine it so,

But the windows are still dirty, and I wonder:
Will it ever end?
The self?
The fixation?

A fool, I persist. In error, I'm afraid.
The sketches made of the straight bend the line.

I react. Patient.
I recede. Longing.
I am, therefor, benign.

Absinthe

In a dazzle of emerald softness, it flew out into the breeze wanting for the red apple in the tree just outside my window. The power had gone out, spare change to total meltdown, and the air inside was stifling, thick with mind-numbing languor and mosquitoes. So I sat on the sill, a wet rag on my forehead, hyacinth blossoms serenading me through a tumbling cloud of exhaust fumes mixed with the stench of rotten garbage from the bins in the alley six stories down. I wanted sleep, wanted surrender, wanted total blackness around me, but it was just too damn hot, too hot even for a wisp of linen.

"Look, Look!" screamed a woman from the street below. "It's the green fairy, I say. Look! Up there!"

I looked around like an idiot, but the only one up here, there, or anywhere was naked ole me, naughty bits a danglin' over the ledge in the moonlight ... well ... just me and my parrot, squawking romantic trifles and tugging at the end of its string.

Road Kill

t was a letdown. Every other weekend and alternating Tuesdays. Miniature golf and fucking drive thrus. Everything's wrapped in wax paper and grease, and the car stinks of French fries and dirty diapers. All those sticky fingerprints on the leather and can we stop now, I have to pee.

This is the last time.
You take a swig.
COFFEE, SODA, WHISKEY.
Wash it down, wash it all away.

It was over. As for Love. You'd forgotten it, of course — *in flagrante delicto.* You used to be proud of that. Admired yourself too long in the mirror, even if she never did.

She never really looked at you.
WINDOWS, WINE GLASSES, REVIEW MIRRORS.
Not once.
Not ever.

You'd had your fears. Your insecurities. That's what she'd always said to you when you were feeling small and frail and useless. That's what she'd use to make sure you owned whatever it was she wanted you to own. Once upon a time, she owned you.
"Daddy, Puppy!"
Yeah, you heard it, the thump and the crunch — a

whimper in the rain — but you just stared straight ahead, at the stop sign, at the potholes, at the moldy French fry in the ashtray.

It was dead. Crawled to the side of the road on two broken legs. You hadn't seen it in the road, behind the car when you pulled out.

The rain.

The headlights.

The sacrifices you had refused to make.

You didn't see it, couldn't possibly see it, and what difference would it make if you refuse to see it now.

"It's just a big rat, sweetie. Wanna go to *McDonalds*?"

The Walls in Our House Were White

My little brother was just a kid, so he didn't put anything into it very often. Maybe a nickel. If he was lucky, a dime or a quarter per week, whatever he had left over from candy and popgun caps. I hated him for doing it. Hated how he carried it around the house all proud of how shiny it was and how it jingled when he shook it. He was a better person than me, and he was just a damn kid, which made the idea of "better" suck even more than it did. I was supposed to be the responsible one, and not for any particular reason that was made clear to me. Just because I was older, like being old somehow granted you superhero powers and shit. My parents are proof that reasoning like that is one-hundred per-cent crap. If I had superpowers, I wouldn't have done it the first time, but the first time felt so good, and not for any particular reason I could make clear to you or to anyone that hasn't yet. Once you do it, it's all you can think about after that: doing it again. So I broke my brother's heart with a hammer and anger and the concrete out in front of the house. Broke it with want not reason. I took everything he had and left him with nothing but rubble. I didn't even feel guilty about it when I did it. He is a better person than me — JUSTIFIED. DONE. — so after the sobbing and the hating of me, he will eventually forgive me. I can wait. The waiting is the only thing that keeps me going, which is why I stand here every Sunday, in the rain, in the ice, and in the snow, staring at a hunk of rock, hoping he can still hear me.

Eating Crow

stabbed a man at the Blue-Buick Bar and Grill. This may not be shocking news, all things considered. The man I stabbed didn't think it was all that shocking, even while it was happening. I'd had a lot of those energy drinks — six or seven — even before I'd puked my grits up on my breakfast plate at that shitty diner down the road. The puke, it was a joke. Doesn't mean I didn't want to take him up on it: the offer. He was nervous and strange, had a lot of flare. Kept at me about positive reinforcement. A little something to help with the ups and downs. He said life was a mystic picnic and that it wouldn't do any harm as long as I knew what was really going on and as long as he knew that I knew. Everyone's gotta be mindful of that shit, he said, even if you're just an addict cruising the bandwidth. It's all just greased wheels and tree trimming and nasty fish splooge appetizers. He said I was full of it when I questioned his motives, and I said, "Who needs a cocktail anyway? Just gimme a beer and let me smoke in the back of the room."

He said, "No." So I stabbed him ... cuz I can get a beer at home.

Them Bones

Bad kids.
Trouble makers.
Lonely, addict-fucker-misanthropes.
The self-proclaimed defilers of what is said to be known.
Anarchists.

They call it a camp, but we never do like in the boy scouts. The Keepers, they make us hate on ourselves for miles in our bare feet, every day, jungle-dragging the dolls behind us on rope we could smoke if we only had matches. We were already whacked from working through the night, the cold and the dark having gnawed at our bloodied fingers. We hate those fucking dolls. They bring them in by the truckload; dump them on the cracked-up concrete out in the yard. We have to pick their stinking carcasses out of the pile, choose them and name them — the ones that would be ours — had to cut out their eyes, burn their hair, shove nails between their tiny painted teeth. We couldn't let them know us or want us. At Christmas time, we'd take the eyes and thread them into garland, hang them over the rusty tetanus-infected mess of rebar that made for a tree. We needed to do these things, and we needed to do what we did alone. Not many stayed for very long, not long to enough to make friends. I had only a few. Jose said his father had tried to choke him out once, and Brad's father shot him with a crossbow while hunting, though it was never determined what exactly his dad had been shooting at. I don't talk about my dad. *Accidents. Prone to.* That's what they called us. But nothing we'd ever suffered in the real world gave us nightmares like the swamp dolls did, barefoot-walking in the murky sludge, carrion fumes rising around us, clinging to the sweat on our skin and on our clothes. It's worse when it rains. They come more when it rains. *The monsters.* They stalk the water, wait for the dolls to come stick-collecting for the evening fires, and when we reach down, the monsters lunge from the depths, tear chunks of flesh to the bone and then drag the dolls down; nothing left behind but mutilated plastic heads, bobbing and floating on the surface. I look out over the swamp. The sky's clear tonight, a warm wind in the trees. I can see farther than the end of history, beyond the farthest of stars. There are hundreds, thousands of heads it seems, swaying in distant moonlit undulations. Adults are liars. They said it was for our own good. Said they loved us. They said when we were done with the program we would be stronger, not the weak, polluted little shits, assholes, delinquents, and jerkoffs we were before we came here.

I don't know if we're any stronger. We strip our clothes off, kneel down in the mud as we pray to Jesus, and then we wade in …

Maybe we are stronger.

Strong enough not to scream.

Sometimes Sandy

Sandy's sad all the time. Sad for no good reason. Punch my fist through the back of her head sad and miserable. All the time. Except when she listens to the radio. She does like to listen to the radio. That's how we met. Over an antique transistor radio. She says it calms her down when she can imagine herself inside the songs, inside even the bad ones. The reds change to blues and the electric whites in her eyes to infinite grays just knowing that in roughly three minutes the story will be over. She says she likes the idea of being over. She's tried. It's not that simple. Me, I want to disappear, slowly, from knowing her. She smiles and then licks her food. And my food. And then she turns to scout out anyone else's food left unattended. It's embarrassing. She chews her nails and dresses for shit too, like an anime schoolgirl sat eating scabs in a fine restaurant next to a giant dung beetle in a billycock and six-fold. I'm the beetle. I try not to look across the table at her. All the food and the booze and the chintz covered walls closing in on her are making her sweat, and she is making me sweat, so I tell her I'm a sailor, then I make a noose from the cooking twine in my pocket so I can pull the half-chewed food out of her throat when she starts choking like she always does in public. Knock. Knock. Who's there? Sandy. Fidgety, sweaty, crazy-eyed Sandy. Or maybe it's the pepper sauce.

"Are you ok?" I ask, but she just shoves a fistful of knuckle into her mouth, so I say it again: "Sandy? Are you ok?"

She thinks there are too many people. In the room. In the world. "It's a Tuesday night. I'm ok, but why are there so many people? That man's elbow is literally in my plate. Do you think they know how crowded it is? The management? It feels crowded, don't you think."

I don't know, and I don't care. What difference does it make that it's Tuesday? She doesn't even know these people. "Can you please just—" I stop myself before I say what I want to say. The waiter fills my wine glass. He's smirking.

Twice Sandy and I had the antibiotic-injected steak and the bitter-almond torte here. Today it's radioactive squid and Vietnamese coffee jelly. Sandy smells like a meadow. The taxi driver has a picture of one on his visor. Old Country. That's my memory of her now, in this moment: a yellow taxi, billowing exhaust fumes on a hill in a Romanian meadow. I stand in the kitchen, feet cold against the tile. Her voice echoes up the staircase, crushes my lungs when I inhale it over the vodka martini in my hand. I'm afraid of what might happen to us if I leave. If I manage somehow to control the twisting and the spinning left without balance, will there still be a Sandy? Will there still be a me? What if? What if she's not lying next to me, drunk, cowering under the covers at three in the morning, will I still want to punch her over the uneaten squid and all those bags of vomit she tries to hide in the basement?

Tries to hide from me.

Molly was a Fucking Tourist

The boys drank in one room.
The girls in another.
Always the same, no matter the letters.
Greek Letters
Shabby sofa on the burnt-out lawn.

Sometimes the lawn was wet and green, and sometimes the sofa was plaid, but not that night. That night, I stood on the lawn thinking that I should have brought a coat but didn't. I thought I might leave to get one, but just as I thought maybe, yes, someone handed me a smile in a red plastic cup, a cramped closet to hide in, and a warm hand to lead me there.

There were rules.

The foyer was for arrivals and introductions. The staircase meant you were easy. Some girls got carried up, kicking and screaming.

Others sobbing.

I heard that a girl came with a padlock on her jeans. She didn't get very far. They held her down and cut those pants off her with a straight razor that one of the kids had stolen from his grandfather's medicine cabinet.

She didn't know the rules. That's what I heard.

I was there that night. The shabby sofa was gold, the lawn muddy, and I'd pushed myself hard into the crowd of shadows, clutched my purse against my chest, and said nothing. Molly was her name. I didn't know her, and it doesn't matter how much *Kool-Aid* you drink or how much *Drano* you snort, you can't make yourself feel something when you just don't feel it. Not scared, not sad, not even the faintest bit guilty for doing nothing. None of us feels anything anymore. I don't think we are supposed to. Shit. The last time I had a good girl cry was when my roommate's fuck-buddy blew chunks all over my bed on the second day of first semester — freshman year. That meant something for some reason, something personal to me at the time. I can't tell you why, only that it hurt a lot, in that quiet space between you and your bones and God, but since then ...

There's nothing.

Molly was just a tourist.

I live here.

I'll be living here the rest of my life.

Cheryl Anne Gardner

One Day We Grow Wings

Cicadas shed their skin as they grow, leaving crisp hollowed-out remains on tree trunks, fence posts, and the undersides of upturned leaves. Tommy and I would collect them in the early morning and stick them to our clothes like brooches.

I used to like Tommy, but I hate him now. He teases me, taunts me now, points to my boobs and yells, "Itty bitty titty committee!" until all the kids in the schoolyard laugh at me. We used to be best friends … until I started to get boobs.

Tommy hasn't grown an inch in four years. There's something wrong with his bones. He told me that's what the nurse had said to his mother, which is why he had to wear those braces on his legs and why he couldn't ride a normal bike that was fast like mine. He told me that before I moved into the neighborhood, he'd had to go to the hospital once. He said he didn't remember much about it, but that when he was brought home, he'd had to lie flat like a mummy for a whole year and that it was very boring and itchy. I didn't think he was fibbing about the story because he is so mean now. I guess lying flat for a year will do that to a person.

On the way home from school today, a cicada flew into my hair. I shook it out and it landed on the sidewalk. It was all shiny new, red eyes and emerald green, buzzing and buzzing, its wings glistening in the sun.

I crushed it; then I ran all the way home.

Desperate Islands are Ours

I find you, sitting in a piazza at a cafe table, alone, a dusky bowl of prime opaque in front of you, served with a side of sticky bacon and gin. "Soon," you say to me, but you always say soon when I'm late, so I tap my foot and wait while squids serenade us from a balcony above; then after a brief violin concerto and a careless "thank you mister" to God for all the small matters he's chosen to ignore, we ride raindrops on eucalyptus dust, lace handkerchiefs crumpled in our pockets. I only fear you when you're near me. I want to tell you that, but just then, the waiter arrives with a stone tablet. You pay the bill with a fist full of coin and ask if the pharmacy's open all night. It is, so you make mental notes in time and shadow while walking behind me in irritation as I foretell the future in condescending rivulets, my rubber boots flip, flap, flopping against a sunset that isn't ours ... and never will be.

Chintz Pickle

What if she doesn't take me seriously?
My sweaty testimony wedged tight behind the tragic I
used to think was honest?
What if, right?
What if …
Isolation
Real men feel that, right?
They have something to say.
Something worth something.
That's what I thought.
What I'd dreamt.

She could make anything look sexy. Even a hammer. I didn't have to dream that, and there ought to be a law against that sort of slant anyway.

But it was late.

Too Late.

And there I was fidgety-vein and chalk-knuckle again, waiting for her on the street. A side street. Could have been any street, but when she appeared, like she always did in her high heels and bare ass, dragging a scuffed-up plastic lawn chair behind her, I pushed my hat up on my brow and lifted my eyes to hers while letting my heart sink as far into the rank of my bowels as I could let it.

We'd been here before, a different street, a mangled guardrail in the distance — MERGE, YIELD, STOP — signs behind us and in front of us diffusing different traffic, different dust, different everything.

She didn't recognize me, but I still missed her. Missed her geometry, her stealth, her madness, and the way the lace slid across her hipbones in the neon truck-stop light. She didn't miss me though. Didn't know me anymore, and so I kept on playing until I heard the coppers hit the bottom of my guitar case.

I'd count it later.

Chump change.

Made her feel less guilty.

Or me more so.

Hey I can make change, too, baby. I can change the chords, change the tempo, change the lyrics completely, but I don't think I can ever change what I've been, on this street, or any other street.

Tin, Tacks, and Tanners … It just is what it is.

It always being the thing in question.

And she didn't miss a thing about me. *No she didn't.* Not like I missed her — the way she used to know me — used to hate me — and so the cars kept passing, and I kept on playing, hoping one day I might change my mind.

Bin Liners are Cheaper at the Hardware Store

I t's a noisy room. Jankety and damp. No open air. People stacked on people stacked on people. A suffocating blur of textures, of thoughts, of multicolored elixirs garnished with opinions non grata. I can't focus on anything. Only his mouth, a mouth I've so wanted on mine. Well, for the last five minutes anyway. The five before that, I wanted the carpet not to be orange shag, and before that, the celery in my Bloody Mary not to be bitter. I often want things like this when I'm in the midst of crowd-sourced terror. The vein in my wrist is throbbing, people can probably see my nipples through this shirt, and his upper lip is sweating spackle into his drink. Am I too close? He can smell the heat on my skin, a hint of honey on my breath. I know he can. *So do it* — I want to say to him — *put your mouth on mine and stop talking.*

I didn't say it though.

I just stare at him, a wounded bird with twisted wings, talons caught in the orange shag, wanting for something real. What can I say? I like the look of him. He's definitely my type: buzz cut bronze with a muscle-stuffed frame, compact, my quarry dove, strewn through his sinews with pride and mud. No pulse. No breath. Just a sense of entitlement drooling from the creases at the corners of his pretty pouty mouth.

For the next five minutes I'll be in love with that

mouth. That black void of ignorance in the middle of his dim … dull … hillbilly face. And I'll be in love with every damn asinine romantic thing comes out of that minty-fresh orifice.

He talks a good game.

Fucks a better one, I bet.

He'll look good wrapped in black plastic.

I want to say that too, but don't.

He nudges my elbow with his, smiles, and then walks his hipster blue-jeans off into the next stupid conversation.

Five minutes always seems like forever.

We'll go to my place after. I probably have more duct tape.

Hiatus Concretion

We roll up top-down-crumpled-clothes-empty to the motor court. It's a relief. We'd been screaming highway days long forgotten, and we both stunk of sweaty vinyl, cigarettes, and licorice. There's so much desert on my teeth that my lips are permanently stuck smiling to them. You wipe yours on your shirtsleeve; smile back at me; tell me I have bugs in mine. I get out of the car, bones creaking in the shifting earth beneath my feet.

Shifting Memories.

Shifting Sand.

A parking lot of sand stretches beyond us, a lone tree clinging to it in the shadow of a snowy mountain range that overshoots the distance so far into the future it seems we might even get there someday. There's a plaid lounge chair next to the tree, a shipping pallet, and a dog tied up, miserable barking in front of the office door, a rot wood screen door, whitewashed, hanging from one rusty hinge. "Like home," you say, then you forty-four the dog in the face. The motel owner doesn't mind. Says he didn't have the heart for it, and the damn dog was an asshole.

The sickness is coming.

I can already see it in you, your hand shaking when you pay the man with a hundred dollar bill. You don't want to let it go, and he isn't sure. Two gnarled hands clasped through sunset over chipped Formica.

I ask him if he has a shovel.

I've never been good at running from things. I let a woman seduce me once at a discotheque. There was something about the way she moved across the dance floor, all quicksilver in crimson, nipples pressed tight against silky fabric. We had a few drinks. She flirted with the bartender, not me, so I told her I liked the way her skin looked against the lights and colored glass. Sparkling. Like she was covered in rhinestones. She wasn't a she though. She was something like me, but more dangerous. She held out her arm. There was barely any flesh on it. Tattooed Bone. Black Market Ivory. The way she looked at me, kissed me in the alley. My Luciana.

It's getting harder to breathe alms in this vortex.

It's getting harder to breathe near you.

"It'll only be a few days," you say, but I know that's a lie. The carpet smells of stale whiskey, and the shower drips chlorinated rust onto the floor. The TV is only black and white, but the bed vibrates — for a quarter. We do that a couple of times, pretend we aren't who we are and giggle until we fall asleep to the coyotes snarling over and tearing at the dog carcass I forgot to bury.

I want to love you.

But I can't.

Origami

When I was five, my Dad would take me to the sawmill. I loved watching the steam engines cloud the sky with pitch. I would stare at them as long as he would let me, as long as it took to feel the soot in my hair. When I got older, he'd take me to the carnival peep shows, and then later, to the whorehouses. Those flashes of small town nipples and heads bobbin' in the dark made me feel like I was someplace else — dark and greasy — someplace I'd never think to get to on my own.

I hate small towns.

Hated being a preacher's son.

Everything was old, tattered, and every day was a day of reckoning. I'd spend my afternoons watching black and white movies. The city folk in those films had fancy cars and chandeliers and never had dust in their homes ... or doubts. My Dad had a lot of things, but he never claimed to have any doubts. Those were for me. When the clock struck seven on a Saturday night, my Dad thought himself a gambling man, his smile a silver bullet wrapped in an Italian suit, his tie the same cornflower blue as his eyes. It was Monte Carlo in the autumn of his life, he said, torrents of gin and jazz flooding the streets with innuendo, loose talk, and loose change. He'd always been a risk taker, a man of charm and chance. If there were a soul to be saved or damned, he'd see it done.

He was a tall man.

A proud man.

No one else saw him that way, of course, but what did it matter? I would think as I watched him stuff a paper flower into his lapel and smooth out his eyebrows with a bit of spit and spirit. All the ladies in the lace push-ups loved him. He'd smoke cigars, wink a lot, and buy everyone rounds of drinks. He laughed and laughed and laughed, the Bible pushing tin against the inside of his jacket, but when he came home, he'd just sit a spell and cry, slumped over the rickety kitchen table with his suspenders hanging loose at his elbows. After he fell asleep, I'd steal into his room and take the paper flower from his lapel. I took every single one until they filled an entire shoebox, which I kept hidden under my bed. They smelled like him. Not the booze or the shoe polish or the grease he put in his hair. They smelled like dirt and old paper, like the psalm books we sang to on Sundays before the freaks, before the whores … before the dust storms left us behind.

It Only Works if You Light It

I imagine you, a cocktail in your hand, an Old Fashioned maybe, something pretentious — something sepia varnished in black and white — as you reluctantly wait for me outside the ladies' room, a smile on your face, the dim light a minute imperfection in your eye as you insult me in front of your friends when I am out of earshot. I called you, but there was no answer. I let it ring four times and then hung up.

It's late. I know. Too late to inventory the streaks in my eyeliner, but I really want to go out. Somewhere maybe anywhere. A bar. A dive. It's cliche, but I really don't care. Just somewhere on the way, out of the way, in the night, in the filthy snow and shadows. I put on stockings; lace up the boots; look at the twists in my legs reflected in the mirror.

It's not about how I imagine you, imagine me, or how I imagine you're with me when you're not or that you might like that cardigan I thought about buying last week but didn't. I called you, but there was no answer. I let it ring six times and then hung up.

I don't drink or smoke. Not when I imagine us together. Lipstick on the glass, I sip the wine slowly now; watch myself smoke in the mirror. The smoke spills over my lips, lifts and frames my face in acid strokes of brutal mystery, but only for a moment. A moment I'll forget in a moment. I called you again, and again there was no answer. I let it ring ten times and then hung up.

When I close my eyes, I think I can feel you, if your hands were here and maybe there.

But I feel empty inside.

And your hands are nowhere.

I called you again, and again, and again. I lost track of the rings and the hang-ups. Lost track of the time.

I think about sleeping, not sleeping, and why I'm not sleeping and maybe you are. I imagine daydreaming about sleeping while watching you twist yourself into the folds of my sheets. Twist yourself into the folds of time I imagine might not be real. I think maybe I could forget you in my dreams? I'd call you again, but I can't find the momentum to do anything except draw the dark down around me. I imagine the cuts will be deeper, simpler. I imagine it all might be easier with than without you ... haunting me.

Spider Cocktails Lilt in Icy Hands

C ast down, your shadowed eyes he tolerates, barely but patiently, as luncheonette counters reflect polished shards of spit and grease into his own. Your voice is an echo, ones and zeros in a noxious void, and it's gotten beyond what he can endure. A lithe back-less twirl in paisley starshine, you will die to him this day. In a moment. A moment of punishment and penance. Of dry aggregate and circles and dandelions and mayhem. You imitate something real, but we are not what we seem. He isn't very good at living, at breathing or kissing you, at walking down brick-clad alleyways in the dark. Isn't very good at bravery or love. Eyeliner heavy on lids, suit starched, your letter, in sweaty hands says "no," the paper wet from the rain, solemn and binding. He looks to the floor, looks beyond you to faux marble, slippery, running in all directions — PAST PRESENT FUTURE — gleaming in the fluorescent sunset slipped through dirty windows, double-glazed so no screams will be heard over the rain drenching neon into the pavement.

He isn't very good in person.

He isn't what he seems.

Antimacassar

S he likes it. Late in the night. Barefoot. Dirty toe-nails in the flickering light from the refrigerator as it bounces against the Three A.M. shadows.

The fridge sweats. The compressor groans. Then rattles for hours in protest ...

And she likes it. Keeps it cold. The liquid icy at first, then warm in her throat and in her chest.

She likes that it's always this way. Three A.M. The fridge light glinting off all the glass and shiny metal.

She likes that it's always just her.

Just a reflection in the kitchen window.

Always this way. The chiffon with sweat clinging,

Always moist.

Always needful.

Dying in the Time

The old man sat there in his tatty armchair, raw knuckles gripping threadbare tight. After a few rounds fresh from the still, he'd gotten himself all fired up about the whole damned mess. "But that's another story," he said and then yelled, "No, woman!" He just wanted to think on things right then, so she just needed to shut her hole and go back in the kitchen.

"Now where was I?" he asked through phlegmy lips and a smoke-rot smile. "Oh yeah. Forgive me, Mister. It's tough to know anythin' for certain, you see. Been too long dyin' in the time," and I might have been a Mister in that moment, but I knew what he meant. Lots of bloody chunks to sift through in that withered old hateful brain of his. You got to feel around in the slurry with your bare hands. Call me *Mister*, call me *Lord of the Flies*, call me whatever, I got a bit of the long road in me too — scorched earth, crossroads, sulphur under my fingernails — so he knew that I knew what he'd done …

He'd seen that car.

Maybe he'd seen it arrive. Maybe not. He said it was "Nobody's business askin'." But I wasn't nobody, and I was asking.

Next time he'd seen it, he said the weeds were already up around it. They grow fast this time of year. Choked that ole barn to rot and ruin in a few months, he said. So he'd seen that car, one of many I'd counted over the years. He'd seen it on his way to work and then again on his way home. "An ole Charger. Rusty bumpers. Paint was chipped up and sprayed over. Matte black. Out of state license plate, somethin' with a bird on it," he thought. "Scrap metal and curiosity, you know." And I did know because I'd seen him when he'd seen it. I wanted to tell him that, scare him just a little for no good reason, but he interrupted me with a: Shut up woman! I'm tryin' to talk here and an offer of hard cider. He said it would give her dumbass something to do. I wasn't thirsty, so he said, "No? Suit yourself, then."

I would, suit myself. I'd pick my teeth with his shin-bone once I got an answer to my question.

Why? That was all I wanted to know, needed to know. Why he'd taken what wasn't his to take, and he replied with a "Well, shit, who knows why. Things get done like that around here. People talk too much. Get it into their heads to go snoopin' around. Then you got yourself a predicament to clean up, so you get an axe, an old sack, stuff the whole fuckin' mess into it, and then roll it down a hill. The ravine over there is steep, the lonely road leadin' up to it long, snarled, and weedy. Crabapples on the ground and nobody around. Nobody watchin'."

But I was watching, a harpoon in my bowtie, a smile on my face. Watching him get the lye, the shovel, the sixty-pound bags of cement. Watching him beg, and pray ... and try to take something that didn't belong to him. "You got to wait after you done it," he said, and I agreed. "After a few weeks it's easier to pull things apart, see. People get what they deserve, Mister. Shouldn't a been out there poking around after dark in the first place."

Cottonwood.

That's the old farm's name. Been deserted for years. Nothing but rats and spooks in those fields now. But down in that ravine, it's quiet. A quiet place for killing. Always has been. It's got some shade from the trees, and you can't hear anything accept the train a few miles away on the ridge come once or twice a day. They say sometimes, right after the train comes, that you can hear the voices, that the place is haunted by the dead folk, covered in blood, swaying from rope in the tops of the trees. "But I never heard nothin' all the times I been down there doin'," he said, and then he justified his confession with, "That water up in there is poison, done run red with crazy. They say that's how it happened. The *Cottonwood massacre*, they call it, but I don't know; the mash tastes fine to me."

Ole Cottonwood Farm …

I remember that day, fondly, a hundred years gone now it seems. It's my lot to remember. That place needed a whole lot of meddling, and the burning lasted weeks. You can still smell it on the air, taste the ash and the hate. The old man said he liked to sit up there a spell after he was done. Sometimes too long. But I know better than anyone that you've got to make sure what's done stays done. He knew it too, said he keeps telling his wife that when she comes a hollering for him in the dark. Fucking kitchen witch, he called her. Said she's just mad because he likes to keep a little something every time, something shiny or something wet and soft. "Things she don't like lookin' at none." That's what she says when she's hollering, but I've been watching them for a while now. That old hag and I go way back; I know her better than he does. She'd boil the skin off a bat for a bit of broom grease, and she's been watching him with those black beady eyes. She's just mad because he doesn't bring anything back for her. That's why I'm here; that's why she summoned me here.

"But somethin' ain't nothin', Mister. A bone, a lock of hair … it's all just scraps," he said leaning towards me through the stench of a righteous whisper, and again, I agreed. But a thief is a thief. A lie is a lie, and once I get done scraping the meat out of his skull with a spoon, he'll get that Cottonwood belongs to me, and in my business, scraps …

Is never just plain ole scraps.

The Followers

Heard the bells in the distance as rain fell hard on the clothesline, revealing strange cast-off patterns in the tatty fabric you'd left to whip in the wind. Withered bone to dark skies held, an afternoon wilted upon your skin.

You'd won the raffle.

Touched the hollow.

The fear lasting, and ugly, a veil of drizzle clouding your eyes, and your breath — swollen — fleeing — I suspect — the lies you'd told, the lies I'd assumed were true. No one spoke of it after that day.

A misfortune, they'd said.

Whispered never to your face.

Eyes wander the streets, away from yours now. Your lot, they'd said as your name was pulled from that rusted iron box. You'll dig the holes tomorrow even though you won't have the strength to finish it. I'll dig again the next day until you do. We'll dig in the darkness and no one will help because it's your lot. To dig them under. We'll do this until *he* comes, netted in shadow, to take them all away to soil sown unseen. You'll get to keep what remains, scorched into dry earth, and I'll tend to that earth alone, weary and blistered from the rot and the heat, because that's my lot. . .

Until the bells toll again,

Until the rain comes,

Until flowers grow frail in the empty spaces.

Dramatic Effect

You wanted transcendence, wanted height, danger, the tracks blurred into murky distances behind and in front of you. You slipped, reached for it, starlight shining in your eyes, something you didn't have when I held your hand.

We didn't fold the laundry this morning, or straighten the tussled sheets. I picked up the mail, but you never opened it.

Yesterday you forgot to buy the raspberry tart I love so much, and I forgot the green tea with jasmine you drink from that old flowery teacup I broke last week and didn't tell you about.

How could I forget your eyes are blue, the concrete beneath you, dingy, muddled with oil.

I hold your hand now and wonder if you can hear me; was there ever a moment you could?

I suspect there was, but there's blood in your hair, and I'm sorry …

I'm sorry for everything: for you, for me, for us.

This Outhouse Reeks

The bathroom had exposed rusty pipework,
A minty lemonade smell,
Ice in the urinal,
And a wall of stone-cold mirror.

She put some lipstick on, but it looked fake under the lint-covered bulb dangling overhead. She wiped off the lipstick but then thought her mouth looked kind of fake, so she pulled out all her front teeth, one by one, and lined them up neatly on the vanity next to the grungy steel soap dispenser.

The teeth looked grungy too,
Maybe from the bad lighting,
And people were banging on the door,
So she slipped her smile into her purse,
One by one.

She thought she might bleach those teeth later ... and see what happens.

Long Sticks
Are Often Useful

I t was just lying there by the side of the road next to a mailbox, pockets turned out, weeds kinda rolled flat around it. I counted three nickels, a dime, and a cigar butt too. I could sure use the change for gum, but I didn't want to get near it. It looked dead, but it just might have been drunk. I don't know anything about dead bodies or drunks. I'm only ten. Some other kids say they'd touched one once: A dead girl. Touched her boobies and everything.

I figure they're lying. We're only ten.

If I Were a Chemist
Not Now
But Maybe In The 1920s

S he said, "I think I'm pregnant," but I thought that the sidewalk looked cleaner than usual, not so many cigarette butts and only a few of those plastic water bottles stuck in the storm drain grate. It was a sunny day but there was snow, in the sky, and on the ground. It was over her, and under her, and soft on her face, the wind whipping it in storm circles, coating the sharp surfaces around us. We'd been here before, walking and talking, like we do, like we did, back when we didn't think about things, didn't calculate distances, or arrival times, or ponder when places would open and close and if people we didn't know would have what we thought we were looking for. We'd been here before. When a walk in the snow was just a walk in the snow. She said, "The snow looks dirty," and all I could think of was my loose shoelace and benzalkonium chloride.

Is That The Kind With Lead In It?

S o there was this bench, wood, birdshit, nothing special about it. Just a bench on which we were sat. Waiting. Fall leaves in a swirling vortex at our feet. Dust and naked trees. Cooing winged rats all around us. Just a bench on a street. Just a girl. Just a guy. I'm the guy, and I had this thought. I'm really no good at thoughts and usually I get what I deserve when I have them. I'm kinda like the bench. She wasn't. She was looking into this little compact mirror, which had been extricated from her handbag with great difficulty only moments before. She was looking into it all squint-eyed as she smeared and smeared and smeared her lips with color. That's when the thought came to me, so I asked, "Why do you, well, why do women put that stuff on their lips?" She stopped her smearing long enough to look at me and smile. Then she went back to the task at hand. Smear, smear, smear, pucker, pucker, pucker, smear, smear, smear. "I don't get it, you know. You have pretty lips. Most women have pretty lips, not that I stalk women's lips or anything. I'm not saying that. I'm just asking." This time I got a smile that was a lot like the bench. She snapped the mirror shut, chucked it and the lipstick into her handbag, and then turned to face me with lips that looked like those huge wax lips you get to eat at Halloween time. I didn't say that though for very obvious reasons, and so there was this little bit of silence until she blew me a kiss with a "You really want to know?" attached to it. I did, and "I do," was my reply because the bench and the birdshit and the pecking rats were all getting on my nerves and I was cold and benches don't get cold, so that was odd, and she just looked at me like I was odd and said, very calmly, "Fellatio. Men like to see the little rings around their peckers when we're done." And that's why I'm the bench and she is not. I wanted to kiss her, had to kiss her. I told her as much, so she asked for a tissue, but then the bus came and she said she couldn't wait for me or the tissue, even if I had one.

Mathilda Is Not My Girlfriend

Some idiot was gonna let a snake eat him. I know, but I saw it on the internets. That's some dumb-assed stuff right there. Everyone knows about snakes. The Jesus book tells us all about them, inside us, slithering through ruby-red and eating our guilt from inside out. It wasn't that Mathilda didn't want that thing she'd never admit to wanting. We don't talk about it. Shame really. That acid cocktail of flat black. I want it too. Ain't afraid to jack the tracks blind for it either. I have no fear of perfection. My apartment smells of crotch, rancid fat, and an act of contrition. It's my signature scent. Mathilda doesn't care. She frequents dark places. Buys stuff at organic markets and talks about Morocco like she'd just unpacked her suitcase yesterday. I'm just ordinary. Non-specific. Never been to Morocco or to Mathilda's place. It's ok though. The snakes give me the strength to endure in spite of my total lack of self-control. Mathilda plays the cello. Lives in a crack-shack near the Jade Fountain take-out. They use snakes and stray cats in their *lo mein*. That fact isn't in the Jesus book, but everyone around here knows those people eat snakes and stray cats. Mathilda says she feels interfered with. Spoiled. From the snakes and the cello and the smell come from the kitchen at that Jade Fountain shithole. She says she wishes that she could just peel her skin off and put it in a scrapbook as a souvenir — for

me. I'd like to taste her skin … and maybe some whiskey. Mathilda says she'd like some whiskey too. I don't
have any though. I don't have a kitchen or a cupboard
or whiskey glasses. All I have is apologies … and rats
and cockroaches and those Jesus snakes in my veins.
Mathilda says she has them too. She picks at hers till
they bleed.

In a Lightning Storm, Sheep Run through Barbed Wire

I used to fear things. The lonesome wind come through the clapboards. Dry hillsides rustling. My own skin in the summer heat. Rattlers. Lurking. Abandoned coal pits. Pa said I was afraid of desolation. I didn't know what he meant by that. How can you be afraid of something all around you been there since the day you were born? I used to. Fear. Hard. But hard is what we had … and the stink of sheep, goats, some cattle and horses. I've seen my sister kicked, bucked, and bloodied more often than I care to remember. Mud in her hair. Booze on her breath. Blue-blackened skin. Used. Useless. Pa used to do the castrations himself. He learned the old-time way and used to use these fucking rubber bands, but he eventually said that the old-time way wasn't the right way anymore, that it took too long, would oftentimes get infected. He feared infections, like the one he said my sister had, so he set about teaching me the right way. I didn't understand why we had to do it at all. It was bloody, and sometimes, the gonads were small, slippery like marbles, and you had to dig around in the sack with your fingers until you found the sinewy cord. Pa would say, "Keep digging," and I'd cry and cry and cry because there was so much blood and I was afraid I'd never get it out from under my fingernails, but

Pa would shush me and tell me that it's good for them, and I'd ask why through a dirty fistful of tears while waiting for him to spit into the chicory and rub his chin for a spell before explaining, the way he does, that boys need it, makes them more polite. Something about hormones, he said. Maybe I was afraid of them, so I asked Ma about it while she was fixing the fried gonads for my supper plate, but she just shushed me too, wiped the grease on her apron, and said I was too young for talk about such things. I'm not too young. My breasts are coming in and I feel all funny. My sister said it's normal. I'd. Get. Used. to it. I go to high school next year. My sister talks about it all the time. Says high school boys have the hormones too. I asked my sister if boys were like the horses and the cattle. She said no. That they were like the mules. I wondered if they stunk like them. She smiled at me and scratched at her crotch, so I told her I was afraid of getting kicked, like she always did, but she shushed me too and said not to worry …

Pa was teaching me the right way.

About the Author

Cheryl Anne Gardner is a writer of dark, often disturbing art-house novellas and abstract flash fiction. Her love of literature began at an early age with Stoker's Dracula. Captivated by the Gothic and Dark Romantic stylings of Poe, Lovecraft, Kafka, and de Sade, her passion for the macabre manifests itself throughout her own work to this day. In 2010, she became enamored with Flash Fiction and its experimental style, and she's been writing prolifically in the genre ever since. She enjoys exploring political, social, and psychological issues. Her flash fiction has been published in dozens of journals. When she isn't writing, she likes to chase marbles on a glass floor, eat lint, play with sharp objects, and make taxidermy dioramas with dead flies. She lives with her husband and ferrets on the east coast USA, is an enthusiastic gardener, and dabbles in cement sculpture when she isn't spoiling her adopted feral cat.

You can find her work at various online retailers. Her novellas are available in print and in eBook formats. Titles include:

The Duskhouse
And Death Dreamt Us All
The Thin Wall
Logos
The Splendor of Antiquity
The Kissing Room

The Credits

A Lukewarm Glass of Milk. *Blue Fifth Notebook.* August 2012.
Absinthe. *Fictionaut.* December 2013.
And Then You Weren't. *Fictionaut.* November 2012.
Antimacassar. *Edge Lit and Other Art.* July 2014.
Bin Liners are Cheaper *Change Seven Magazine.* March 2015.
Blowout. *Literary Orphans, Issue 1 - Babe.* May 2012.
Broken. *Downer Magazine, Volume 1-3.* 2012.
Candlelight Vigils. *Gay Flash Fiction.* June 2013.
Chintz Pickle. *Fictionaut.* March 2014.
Communion. *Fictionaut.* November 2013.
Debt Collectors. *The Carnage Conservatory.* July 2012.
Desperate Islands are Ours. *ExFic.* March 2014.
Ditch Diggers Tend Picket Fences. *Change Seven Magazine.* 2015.
Dramatic Effect. *Fictionaut.* July 2014.
Dying in The time. *Near to The Knuckle* April 2015.
Eating Crow. *Fictionaut.* January 2014.
Espresso. *The Carnage Conservatory.* February 2013.
Gekkonidea. *The Legendary.* March 2015.
Glass Houses. *Fictionaut.* June 2012.
Gourmet Meat Haters. *Cease, Cows.* June 2013.
Hiatus Concretion. *Metazen.* June 2014.
Hula-Hoops, Boys, and Bottle Rockets. *Salt.* May 2012.
If I Were A Chemist... *Fictionaut.* October 2014.
In a Lightning Storm... *Revolution John.* December 2014.
Ink. *Fictionaut.* February 2013.
Is That The Kind With Lead In It? *Lit Bulb Festival.* May 2015.
It Only Works if You Light It. *Danse Macabre du jour.* April 2014.
Kitsch. *The Molotov Cocktail.* September 2012.
Long Island Iced Tea. *The Carnage Conservatory.* June 2012.
Long Sticks Are Often Usefull. *Fictionaut.* September 2014.
Making Dinner on Mars. *69 Flavors of Paranoia Menu #18.* July 2012.
Mathilda Is Not My Girlfriend. *Fictionaut.* November 2014.

Molly was a Fucking Tourist. *Vagabond City Lit.* February 2014.

One Day We Grow Wings. *Fictionaut.* February 2014.

Origami. *Americana.* s.l., Synaesthesia Magazine, May 2014.

Parachuting in Stilettos. *Linguistic Erosion.* February 2013.

Road Kill. *Black Heart Magazine.* January 2014.

Skinned Rabbits. *Yellow Mamma.* October 2013.

Sometimes Sandy. *BareBack Magazine.* March 2014

Sometimes Things Just Are… *Fictionaut.* December 2012.

Spider Cocktails Lilt in Icy Hands. *Postcard Shorts.* May 2014.

Taking Lives. *Micro Horror.* March 2013.

The Followers. *Foliate Oak.* March 2015.

The LongPig. *The Carnage Conservatory.* October 2013.

The Mission Box. *The Rogues Gallery: Illustrated Police News.* s.l., Firbolg Publishing, 2014.

The Walls in Our House Were White. *Fictionaut.* December 2013.

Them Bones. *The Molotov Cocktail.* January 2014.

This Outhouse Reeks. *Fictionaut.* August 2014.

Under New Management. *Fictionaut.* December 2013.

Unexpected Guests. *One Title Magazine.* September 2012.

What Do We Do With The Silence? *Literary Orphans, Marilyn.* April 2013.

AND DEATH DREAMT US ALL
A Novella

Her prose is full of lyricism and imagery that you will find both stunning and disturbing. — Amazon

The imagery is sublime, the tension palpable. If you love dark fiction, you gotta get this book. — Bolt Cutter Design

Rowan is one deliciously haunted individual and the prose proves both dark and inviting. — Amazon

LOGOS
A Novella

Gardner's words kindle fires in the reader similar to dark woeful wordsmiths like Anne Rice and Poppy Z. Brite. Packs a powerful wallop. — Horror.com

Immersion into Gardner's macabre settings is inevitable for the reader. — BreeniBooks.com

A dark and richly detailed work. — Amazon

THE THIN WALL
A Novella

Both literary and erotic without being tacky or over-indulgent. — PODBRAM

Dark almost obsessive eroticism in the most romantic of tones. Convincing and unashamed. — Goodreads

A story that is both entertaining and frightening at the same time. — DactylReview

www.ingramcontent.com/pod-product-compliance
Lightning Source LLC
Chambersburg PA
CBHW071333130626
46556CB00004B/1882